Clara Vu

Dotty
DETECTIVE

HarperCollins *Children's Books*

First published in Great Britain by HarperCollins *Children's Books* 2016
This edition published in the USA by HarperCollins *Children's Books* 2017
HarperCollins *Children's Books*
is a division of HarperCollins*Publishers* Ltd,
1 London Bridge Street, London, SE1 9GF

The HarperCollins website address is: www.harpercollins.co.uk

20 LSC/H 10 9 8 7 6 5 4 3 2

Text and illustrations © Clara Vulliamy 2016

ISBN 978-00-0-824370-8

Clara Vulliamy asserts the moral right to be identified as the
author and illustrator of the work.

Printed and bound in the USA

Find out more about HarperCollins and the environment at
www.harpercollins.co.uk/green

This book is for Martha
because we love her so much

Read the whole series:

★ *Dotty Detective*

★ *Dotty Detective: The Pawprint Puzzle*

★ *Dotty Detective: The Midnight Mystery*

★ *Dotty Detective: The Lost Puppy*

This book
belongs to...

DOT

and McClusky

This is me!

My real name is Dorothy Constance
Mae Louise. I am named after two
grandmas, an auntie, and my mom's
pet rabbit when she was little.

But everybody calls me Dot.

This is McClusky. I am his very best pal.

We moved into our new apartment today— me, the twins, McClusky, and Mom.

DOT'S ROOM

Right now I am in my new bedroom!

My stuff is mostly still in boxes, but I manage to find my best pyjamas with flamingos on them, AND my extra-tricky puzzle book for bedtime.

McClusky is running around and around smelling every single new thing and barking. You're a CRAZY GUY, McClusky!

I'm snuggled down in bed now, wide awake. I can't close the curtains because there aren't any yet.

Tomorrow is my first day at Oakfield School. I am REALLY excited—I am sure it's going to be amazing. But I won't know A SINGLE PERSON, which gives me a fluttery butterfly feeling inside.

I know just what I need. I jump out of bed, searching for—

my sparkly red
LUCKY SHOES!

10

I'll just put them here...

...ready for the morning.

MONDAY

Today's the day!

EEK! My hair looks like THIS:

EERGH!

Total chaos in the kitchen. Everybody rushing. I grab some toast. Mom says, "Pick up your lunchbox and good luck and be friendly and wipe that toothpaste off your sweater!"

OOPS!

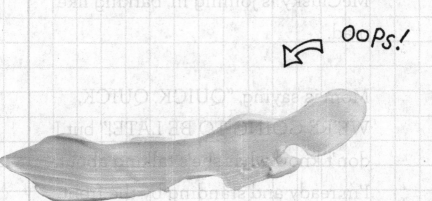

The twins are shouting a made-up
song they think is hilarious, and
McClusky is joining in, barking like
mad.

Mom is saying, "QUICK, QUICK,
WE'RE GOING TO BE LATE!" but I
don't know what she's talking about.
I'm ready and standing by the front
door.

Hurrying to school. We have to walk very fast. I am a TOTAL BLUR.

But I feel GOOD in my red lucky shoes!

McClusky whines and whimpers at the school gate. He is going to miss me a LOT.

In my new classroom!

Laura Drew
Amy Trotter
Frankie Logan
Beans
me

My teacher is Mr. Dickens. His eyes
are a bit googly and he is very smiley.
If he had a tail, he'd be wagging it.

Mr. Dickens says, "YAY! This is Dot. She's the new kid in town—everybody say HI!"

He talks in a way I was not expecting AT ALL.

On my table there is Frankie Logan, who wriggles all the time and tips his chair. "You've got ants in your pants, Frankie Logan!" says Mr. D.

There is Amy Trotter, who is quiet and has very neat braids.

And there is Laura Drew. She has glittery pens with fluffy pompoms on top. Her friends have them, too, exactly the same.

I sit next to a boy who is called BEANS even though his real name is Ben.

I ask him why everybody calls him that. He says it's because he likes beans! Oh, OK!

My pencil case has ducks wearing shower caps on it. Mom says it's really a sponge bag, but they are the same thing and no one will notice.

"That's a sponge bag," says Laura Drew.

Recess. Eating my pineapple slices
and exploring in the playground.
I can't see anyone from my class
because it's so crowded.

In Math, which I'm good at, Mr. D.
looks at my worksheet and says,
"FAB!"

Lunchtime. Most of my class are sitting
in groups already. I find an empty

seat. Having my lunch and doing a wordsearch in my puzzle book.

After lunch, Mr. D. tells us about the school CLUBS. There is:

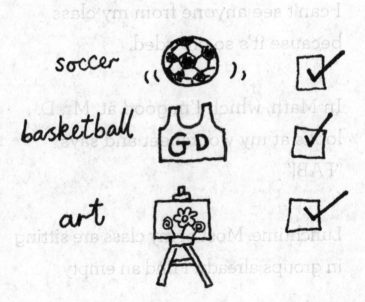

soccer ((⚽)) ✓

basketball 👕GD ✓

art 🖼️ ✓

karate  ☑

knitting ☑

choir ☑

I join them ALL.

PHEW LOOOOOOOOOOOOOO

OOOOOONG DAY...

For dinner we have curry straight out of the foil dishes because we can't find any plates with all the unopened boxes.

Later, I squeeze through my bedroom door, which can only open a little bit because of all the boxes still piled up. I unpack more of my stuff.

Hello, stuff!
I've got the BEST collection of stickers and polka-dotted notebooks and

special pens and different kinds of
string, and paperclips in every size and
color. Mom says I have a stationery
obsession bordering on SEVERE.

While I'm arranging my collection and sorting out my desk, I think about my first day at Oakfield School. I guess it's like when we first got McClusky and he needed time to get to know his new home. (Not that I'm like McClusky was then – he went berserk when he first heard the vacuum cleaner, and hid under the couch for three days!)

I KNOW I'm going to really love it. I just need time to settle in.

And to settle into my new room, too. It's very plain so I think about how I'd

like to decorate it. I start jotting down a
few ideas...

Mom says we will have to save up for
the chandelier, and the revolving door
is a NO-NO.

Tuesday

The twins (Alf and Maisy) have cereal boxes on their heads and are pretending to be robots.

They are so noisy it's hard to believe there are only two of them—I can't help laughing.

Mom says, "HURRY UP! WE'RE GOING TO BE LATE AGAIN!" but now she can't find her keys.

I'm excellent at finding things. Here they are, under McClusky's dribbled-on squeaker.

Nice cat on the corner of our street!

Oops too quick—missed it!

But anyway, that's a LUCKY SIGN.
It's going to be a good day.

Lining up to go into our classroom...

Laura says she is starting a club, but
it is INVITATION ONLY. She has a
glittery pink notebook for the club
rules.

Amy is looking like she doesn't mind
whether or not she's invited (she isn't),
but I think maybe she does.

In Science, we are doing weather.

Mr. D. tells us about air pressure and does a TERRIFIC experiment with a milk bottle and a boiled egg.

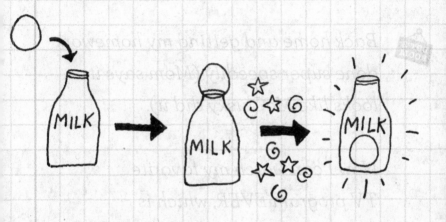

Lunchtime. Having my lunch and doing a tricky maze in my puzzle book.

In Computer Science Frankie Logan

sticks a rubber spider's leg up his nose and now he has a nosebleed. "CALAMITY CUSTARD!" says Mr. D.

Back home and getting my homework done super-speedily (Mom says it looks like McClusky did it).

Now I can watch my favorite TV program EVER, which is **FRED FANTASTIC — ACE DETECTIVE.**

There are lots of dastardly villains on the mean streets of the big city, getting up to mischief. It's up to Fred

Fantastic to put a stop to them.
Fred Fantastic has a brown raincoat
and wears his hat down over his face
so he is very mysterious and shadowy.

He has a cool sidekick called Flo and
she is fantastic, too.

They may be fantastic ... but I'm even
better! I can always solve the crime
before they do.

Fred Fantastic is also a **hard-boiled gumshoe.**

This is nothing to do with eggs or chewing gum stuck to your foot. It means he's a tough guy who does his detecting stealthily with quiet shoes.

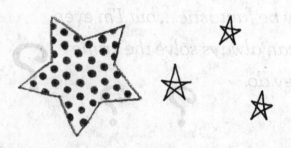

Wednesday

Mom says, "I AM LITERALLY TEARING MY HAIR OUT" (but she isn't, literally) "BECAUSE WE WILL BE LATE AGAIN!"

But now we are waiting while she finishes an email.

I pull my hoodie out from underneath McClusky and we rush out of the front door. But I am looking *slightly* hairy.

Lining up to go into our classroom I realize, OH NO, Mom hasn't given me 20 cents for the charity cupcake sale!

On the way to assembly, Beans says he watches

FRED FANTASTIC — ACE DETECTIVE

too, and he thinks it is — GENIUS.

"Fred Fantastic has loads of cool adventures," says Beans. "Why doesn't anything exciting ever happen around here?"

Assembly is Mrs. Bagshott showing hundreds of photos from her bicycling holiday.

Actually, hundreds AND HUNDREDS.

At recess, Beans buys a cupcake and gives me a bit. We sit together at lunch.

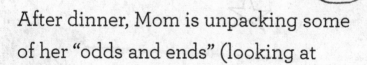

After dinner, Mom is unpacking some of her "odds and ends" (looking at her collection of egg cups, I think it's more like just "odds").

I still have to squeeze through the gap in my bedroom door and it is STILL chaos everywhere. But I don't care about any of that. I think about how it's going to be good at Oakfield School. I've got a friend!

THURSDAY

At registration, Mr. D. says he will make **AN ANNOUNCEMENT** later. Everyone is talking at once about what it will be.

At nearly home time, Mr. D. says, "In three weeks' time..." (he is doing a little dance).

"There will be..." (he is doing SUSPENSE).

"A SCHOOL TALENT SHOW!"

"Hooray!" says almost everybody.

"There's no way I'm doing that," says Beans.

Mr. D. says EVERYONE has a special talent. He is going around the room, asking people what they could do.

Joe Buckley says he will cut someone in half for a magic trick, and Kirstie Brown says she will do her tap dancing.

Fiyaz says he can raise one eyebrow.

(HE CAN!!!)

Laura Drew says she will sing and her friends will do backing vocals, which means they will stand at the back.

Amy says she would like to sing, too, but she says it very quietly.

40

I can see Laura and her friends whispering and looking over at Amy. I'm wondering what they are saying.

Luckily the bell goes before Mr. D. gets to me, as I don't know what my special talent is! DO I EVEN HAVE ONE???

After school, I lie on my bed and I think about the talent show.

Some talents happen onstage with lights and people clapping. Other talents happen in your head and are not really the clapping-for kind.

I make a list of all the things I am good at (I am good at lists!):

puzzles

fast running

finding things

brushing tangles out of McClusky's coat

math

eating three super-sour apple candies at once

42

WORD SEARCH

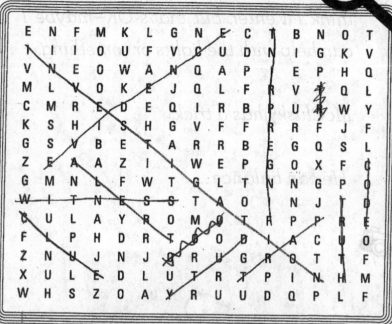

E	N	F	M	K	L	G	N	E	C	T	B	N	O	T
T	I	I	I	O	U	F	V	U	D	N	I	G	K	V
V	N	E	O	W	A	N	Q	A	P	E	P	H	Q	Q
M	L	V	O	K	E	J	Q	L	F	R	V	R	Q	L
C	M	R	E	D	E	Q	I	R	B	P	U	R	W	Y
K	S	H	I	S	H	G	V	F	F	R	R	F	J	F
G	S	V	B	E	T	A	R	R	B	E	G	Q	S	L
Z	E	A	A	Z	I	I	W	E	P	G	O	X	F	C
G	M	N	L	F	W	T	G	L	T	N	G	P	P	T
W	I	T	N	E	S	S	T	A	O	T	N	J	T	D
O	U	L	A	Y	R	O	M	O	T	R	P	P	R	E
F	L	P	H	D	R	T	O	O	D	I	A	C	U	O
Z	N	U	J	N	J	Q	R	U	G	R	O	T	T	F
X	U	L	E	D	L	U	T	R	T	P	I	N	H	M
W	H	S	Z	O	A	Y	R	U	U	D	Q	P	L	F

WORD LIST

~~WITNESS~~   ~~EVIDENCE~~
~~CLUE~~   ~~INVESTIGATION~~
~~GAP~~   ~~TRUTH~~
   ~~CODE~~
   ~~FINGERPRINT~~

Search the puzzle above to find 10 detective words from the word list.

CLUE !!

The words are in all directions—vertical, horizontal, diagonal and even backwards!

See, I'm a puzzle whizz-kid!

I can't really do these in a show. I don't think I'll enter, but that's OK—maybe I can help with the lights or something.

McClusky has a trick.

He can balance...

absolutely...

ANYTHING...

on his head.

It's a shame he can't enter!

FRIDAY

At recess, Amy tells Beans and me that she would like to sing "Over the Rainbow" from **THE WIZARD OF OZ** in the talent show.

I say, "Great! I love **THE WIZARD OF OZ**. That Dorothy is my favorite Dorothy apart from me. And I love her dog, Toto, too."

Amy says, "But I am so nervous! I am not a super-confident person." She looks over at Laura, then looks at the floor.

Laura is standing nearby and I know she is listening.

Grandpa George picks me up from school. He always brings me a candy bar.

Mom says I should remember to check the sell-by-date with Grandpa

George's candy bars because he keeps them for YEARS.

This one is OK. It just smells a bit of old cupboard.

SATURDAY

Waffles! YESSS!!!

Alf and Maisy are talking to each
other in their secret twinny language.
Mom says thank goodness for a
sensible conversation with me.

Having a nice lazy day.

In my room, I am painting my toenails

49

in different colors—violet, orange, blue, violet, orange, blue ... and I paint dots on my fingernails.

I wanted to wear my rainbow socks that Mom says are too small for me (it is true they make my toes curl over, but I say that's cosy!) but they have disappeared —very odd.

And I'm thinking about quiet Amy, and about super-confident Laura Drew.

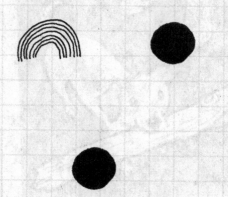

SUNDAY

Me, the twins, Grandpa George, and Mom take McClusky for a walk. He insists on carrying a really big stick. Actually it is more of a tree trunk.

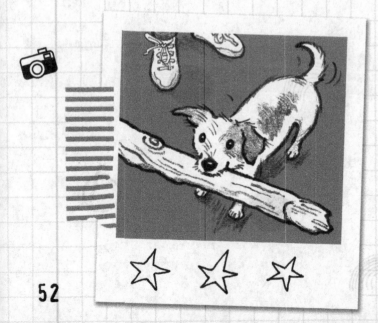

You'll never get through that gate, McClusky—what are you going to do now?!

Mom asks me about school and I tell her I have a friend called Beans. She says I should ask him over for dinner tomorrow after school.

Monday

"A new week!" says Mom at breakfast. She turns over the page on our wall calendar and it says "work hard, dream big!".

In the playground before school, Mom and I find Beans and his dad and arrange for Beans to come over for dinner.

Lining up to go into lunch, Amy says

she has been practising her song all weekend and wonders if she is brave enough to enter the talent show.

I look down at my lucky shoes. They are VERY LUCKY, plus they are red and sparkly, just like Dorothy's shoes in **THE WIZARD OF OZ**.

I have an idea…

I say, "Amy, you can borrow my LUCKY SHOES. They'll help you to be brave!"

Amy is so pleased she does a happy

squeak like a guinea pig, which
makes me giggle.

Laura looks over at me and Amy and
frowns.

Then, when I am leaving the lunch hall, I can hear Laura on the other side of the lunchbox trolley, talking with her friends.

She can't see me, but I have **COMPLETELY CLOCKED** her. This is something Fred Fantastic would say.

She is whispering, "I'M going to win the talent show, NOT Amy, and I have a PLAN."

A PLAN?!?!

I do not like the sound of this one bit.

WHAT IS SHE UP TO???

In class in the afternoon, we are
doing quiet reading.

I whisper to Beans that there's
something FUNNY going on with
Laura, and although I don't think he
has really noticed he whispers "YES,
THERE IS."

I tell Beans what Laura said about
Amy and having **A PLAN.**

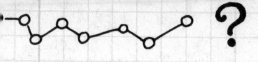

"I don't know what's going on, but I don't like it one bit!" I say.

"What can we do?" says Beans.

"We can be super-sleuthing detectives like Fred Fantastic," I say, "and get to the bottom of this murky mystery!"

Beans thinks this would be completely amazing. **Hooray!**

"QUIET READING, chatterboxes!" says Mr. D.

After dinner — and after the twins have forced me and Beans to play at least one billion games of hide-and-seek—we escape to my room to talk about how we are now ace detectives too!!!

"Our detective agency will be me, you, and also TOP DOG McClusky, because there's no point in trying to stop him joining in if he's determined to," I say.

McClusky barks as if to say, "No point at all!"

"Now all we need is a name," I say.

We talk about Fred Fantastic's FIVE GOLDEN RULES for being an ace detective …

 STAY FROSTY.
This means STAY ALERT.
Fred Fantastic says this a lot.

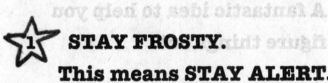 **FOLLOW THAT HUNCH!**
Always listen to your instincts because it could lead to something.

USE YOUR NOODLE.
Use your brain—think!

 LOOK FOR A LIGHT-BULB MOMENT.
A fantastic idea to help you figure things out.

GET PROOF.
You always need evidence before coming to any crafty conclusions.

"Solving a case is like a really complicated joining-the-dots puzzle,"

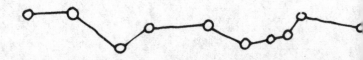

I say. "Connect the clues and get the answer!"

"Join the Dots Detectives!" says Beans. "That would be a TERRIFIC name!"

So now my bedroom is:

Join the Dots Detectives HQ

I'm going to write down all the clues we find, then together we will deductivize what exactly is going on,

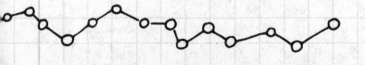

however fiendishly mysterious!
This calls for my special pens, and—
AT LAST!—I can use my Ace Detective
Stamp Set, starting with …

...which this book will now be!

Our only clue so far in the **LAURA AND THE TALENT SHOW MYSTERY** *is "looking"...*

It's not much to go on yet, but whatever your PLAN is, Laura Drew— WE'RE ON THE CASE!

Laura is writing in the pink glittery notebook and her INVITATION-ONLY-CLUB friends are looking and smiling.

I say to Beans, "We MUST see inside Laura's notebook! I have a hunch there will be a vital clue in it."

"That will be VERY tricky," says Beans. "She keeps it in her pocket at all times."

"**STAY FROSTY**, Beans!" I say.

Throwing and catching skills in Gym. Beans does not catch the ball a single time because he is concentrating so hard on staying frosty.

In Math, Laura's notebook slides off her lap and on to the floor. THIS IS OUR CHANCE! Me and Beans subtly dive for it at the same time...

...and—**OUCH!**—bang heads. I can see stars! Quick as a flash, the notebook is back in Laura's pocket.

At lunch, Beans says, "Badges! We need badges to show we are Join the Dots Detectives!"

"What a great idea, Beans!" I say.

As soon as I'm back at HQ,, I waste no time in getting down to my badge-making. It is vitally important that they are super-secret so they do not BLOW OUR COVER. This means being found out when you are on a detecting mission. Fred Fantastic says this a lot, too.

I cannot find my zigzag scissors.

Strange—did I leave them behind in our old house?

But I DO use my BEST polka-dot stickers.

I'm pretty pleased with the result...

McClusky can't have a badge because he'd probably eat it.

Sorry, McClusky!

I watch **FRED FANTASTIC—ACE DETECTIVE.** There's a really good bit where he solves the whole case just by finding half a bus ticket.

Dinner is peas and rice. **YUM!** There is completely NO SUCH THING as too many peas in my life.

And the twins cannot have too many peas in their hair either!

Beans LOVES our Join the Dots
Detectives badges! We pin them
under our coat collars so no one can
see.

We are stepping up our **TOP SECRET
SUPER-SLEUTHING** operation, and find
a good place for a Lookout.

When the grounds-keeper Mr. Meades

goes past, we pretend we are looking
in an interested way at some soil.

the playground

our
lookout

the
hall

nature corner

where Laura's
invitation-only
club meets →

class-
rooms

↑
sports
equipment
crate

After lunch, Amy asks Beans and me if we will be an audience while she practises her song.

At first she is all quavery with nerves, but when she gets going—**WOW!**

"I can see why Laura is worried that Amy will win," I whisper to Beans.

"We just have to make sure her singing goes to plan," Beans agrees.

I'm heading out of the school gate at home time (me, the twins, and Mom), when I see Laura in front of me, and ...

... a piece of paper falls out of her pocket!

I pick it up and put it in my bag.

Rushing home because I really need to examine it further.

In through the front door—but—
LOOK AT OUR SOFA!! McClusky
has done THIS to a cushion...

McClusky's guilty face!

I help Mom to clear up after
McClusky, but really quickly, because
I'm in a HUGE HURRY to get to HQ.

AT LAST I can have a private look at our first proper clue.

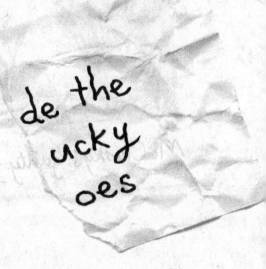

But it's nothing. SO disappointing.

I throw it at the bin in the corner of my room.

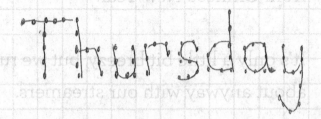

Thursday

We are going on a school trip!

Mr. D. says we will be intrepid explorers and experience weather in the wild. We walk up the hill to the local park with our clipboards.

Our task is to measure the wind using our homemade windsocks, streamers, and a paper fish left over from Chinese New Year.

It's only a little bit breezy, but we run about anyway with our streamers.

We look for different cloud formations until it's time to walk back. I LOVE cloud-gazing.

Lunchtime. Really distracted from my cheesy dip and carrot sticks, even though they're my favorite, because Laura is STARING at my lucky shoes.

I think she is jealous because she loves sparkly things.

In Knitting Club. Beans isn't that keen on knitting, but he is so desperate to talk detective that he is going to try a scarf.

"Fred Fantastic has loads of cool gadgets," says Beans.

We think about what we would have in our ideal detective kit. Walkie-talkies, night-vision goggles, a pen with a hidden camera, scuba-diving suits...

Beans says he can make a periscope out of toilet-paper rolls for looking around corners.

I say, "What we really need is a SECRET CODE. To tell the other person when we have urgent news! I will think of something. I love codes."

While I have my dinner, I look in my

puzzle book. There are codes here, but none are quite right.

Mom has bought lots of pink wafer biscuits from the market because they are the twins' favorite, and also because they are very cheap.

I put one—two—three on my plate.

(Oh, all right, McClusky, you can
have half.)

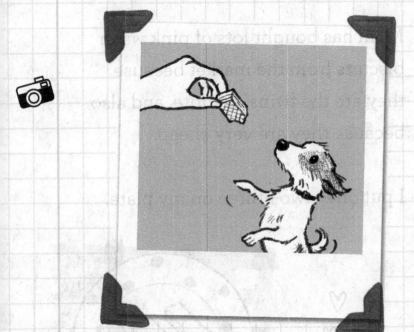

I am beginning to have a terrific idea...

Friday

Before the bell goes for lining up,
I say to Beans, "I've been USING
MY NOODLE and I've now had
a **LIGHT-BULB MOMENT:**
the Pink Wafer Code!"

I show Beans a chink in the wall next
to the school gate. "We leave one or
two or three pink wafers in the chink
if we have important news to tell each
other," I say.

The **Pink Wafer Code** works like this:

One means: We need to talk.

Two means: Urgent.

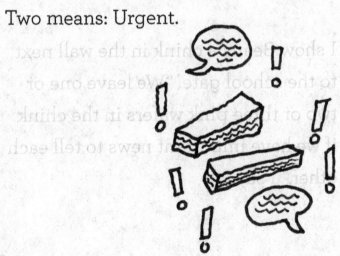

Three means: **TOTALLY LIFE—AND—DEATH EMERGENCY—COME STRAIGHTAWAY!!**

It's fiendishly clever, because we can eat the evidence afterwards.

In class, Laura is bursting loudly into
song and flinging her arms wide,
looking at her reflection in the window.

Amy is even quieter than usual. She
spends a long time looking in her
bag, but doesn't take anything out.

In English, we are writing poems
about WEATHER DISASTERS—
hurricanes, tornados, tropical storms,
coastal flooding.

Beans whispers that it's funny that
hurricanes have girl's or boy's names,

and if there
was a Hurricane
Laura, you would need
a **BIG**
umbrella.

Frankie Logan says he likes the
"storm devil" best, and knocks over
his chair doing an impression of it.

Mr. D. says that we are so noisy today
he is hoping for a cyclone to take
us all home so he can have a quiet,
peaceful weekend.

SATURDAY

SATURDAY

SATURDAY

Me and Mom go for a run, and Alf and Maisy go to the adventure playground with Grandpa George.

We all have a take-out hot choc from the van.

I help Mom give the twins their bath because she is tired and bath time is seriously chaos. Water **EVERYWHERE**.

SATURDAY

SATURDAY

While the twins are having their hair washed and it's all bubbly, I give them funny hairstyles and me a funny beard. They giggle hysterically.

This brings McClusky rushing in to see what's going on, because he absolutely cannot bear to miss out on any fun.

At last McClusky is in his basket and the twins are asleep, so me and Mom have one of our special film nights.

Mom falls asleep ten minutes in, wakes up at the end and says, "That was LOVELY!"

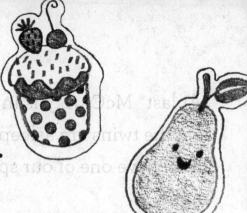

Sunday

Mom AND McClusky are both on a diet again. This usually means whining next to the treats drawer (McClusky) and sighing with a salad (Mom).

At lunch, McClusky is following my fork with his eyes from plate to mouth and back to plate. Looks utterly miserable. LONGING for a sausage.

Nothing else to report. My things are mostly unpacked now, but everything still looks a bit empty AND my door handle keeps falling off.

*So I do more doodling on my hopes
for my nice new room. A Jacuzzi
would be good...*

me   twins   Mom   McClusky

I see that Beans has put two wafers in the chink.

Before lining-up time, he shows me the periscope he has made for our detective kit! It has two little mirrors inside. Beans is SO CLEVER.

97

Recess. Me and Beans are in The Lookout with our new periscope.

It works! We see Laura go past. She walks over to the playground equipment crate and looks behind it.

That doesn't seem interesting or important, so after a bit we stop watching and talk about our favorite **FRED FANTASTIC** episodes instead.

Mr. D. tells us that after school tomorrow there's a talent-show rehearsal.

Anyone not performing can be in the Support Crew. Mr. D. says that the Support Crew are superstars, too. Me and Beans put our names down.

When I get in from school, I dig out my special **FRED FANTASTIC'S CRAZY CRIME CAPERS** book and put it in my bag to show Beans tomorrow.

(It might help us have more **LIGHT-BULB MOMENTS**.)

For dinner, Mom makes baked-potato surprise. It is a baked potato cut in half and mashed up with butter and cheese and put together again.

We have this a lot, so it's not much of a surprise.

TUEsdAy

At lunchtime, me and Beans look at **CRAZY CRIME CAPERS**.

Beans likes the section on false beards best, but I'm not sure how that will help us solve the great **LAURA AND THE TALENT SHOW MYSTERY**.

Me and Beans stay after school to help with the rehearsal. Amy tries on my sparkly red shoes and they fit perfectly. Suddenly she is smiling.

Mr. D. says that all of the acts are great but some need just a little more polish.

"You could take someone's eye out with that yo-yo, Marcus!" says Mr. D.

"You can't JUST raise one eyebrow, Fiyaz! Do you know any jokes?"

The school stereo doesn't seem to be working very well and the music keeps jumping.

When it's Amy's turn to sing, it doesn't work at all, just makes a crackling noise. Amy is not smiling now—she is nearly crying. Poor Amy.

And who should be sitting right next to the stereo, offering to help, which she NEVER usually would …

LAURA DREW!!!

She is slightly smiling, too.

Hmmmmmmmmmmm…

Back at HQ and I have some vital **TOP SECRET** *detective thinking to do.*

In fact, I have a very detectively HUNCH that Laura's sudden interest in the stereo is another clue...

I am brushing McClusky's hair. It helps me think.

And I suddenly realize something else.
It isn't just my shoes Laura is jealous
of. She is jealous of Amy, because Amy
is a nice person with a lovely voice and
friends who lend her their lucky shoes
for good luck.

Tonight's **FRED FANTASTIC** episode is
all about the fifth golden rule of being
an ace detective—you can't build a
case without solid PROOF.

WEDNESDAY

At lunchtime chess club, I try not to win too quickly because me and Beans need time for a private conversation.

"My hunch is telling me it's all about the school stereo, Beans!" I say. "Laura must be planning to sabotage Amy's song. But we've got to **GET PROOF**."

"Keep your eyes peeled and **STAY**

FROSTY!" says Beans.

We try and try ALL DAY.

In class, we casually saunter past Laura's chair and look over her shoulder, hoping for even the tiniest glimpse at her pink glittery notebook.

But our sauntering is TOO casual and we knock over the pencil holders. It takes ages to pick them all up again.

At playtime, we hide close to where Laura's INVITATION-ONLY club

meets, peering through the bushes,
trying to hear what they are saying...

But no luck. Laura is keeping her
plans UNDER WRAPS.

At lunch, we plan to sit near Laura's
table and eavesdrop...

But she gives us such a cross look we
don't dare and we rush with our lunch-
boxes to the other side of the lunch room.

Mostly they are just listening to Laura
talking about her skiing holiday.

Aargh!!!

Later on in Art, we are doing weather pictures.

Amy paints the tornado from **THE WIZARD OF OZ** and Dorothy's house landing on The Wicked Witch of the East with only her legs sticking out.

Mr. D. says, "WOW, Amy, you have really painted that squashed witch with FEELING."

Me and Beans are working together.

We have an artistic idea that I can only describe as PURE GENIUS, involving colored paper and lots of glitter.

But at home time when we are fetching our bags, I see THIS:

I run to catch up with Beans.

"Now we have all the PROOF we need—Laura is even taking the stereo home so she can make sure it doesn't work for Amy on the day!"

Beans is really fuming and says, "Well, that **TAKES THE CAKE!** We must DO something!" We agree to tell Mr. D. first thing tomorrow.

It takes FOREVER to get home from school, because Alf and Maisy insist on walking the entire way backwards.

But I join in and walk backwards, too,

and then so does Mom. McClusky
looks at us like HE'S the sensible one,
which is funny coming from him.

*In my room, I look around. Something
feels different, but I'm not sure what…*

*Hey! That's strange—there's a picture
of me and McClusky missing from my
pinboard…*

Tonight as I eat my dinner, it doesn't
feel like butterflies in my tummy—
more like a huge churning cement
mixer.

Mom is busy with the twins so I decide not to tell her about Laura and the stereo—besides, me and Beans have got it under control.

I wonder if it will be like one of Fred Fantastic's **GRAND REVEALS**, when he gathers everybody together in one room and points to the villain. There are usually gasps and open mouths because everyone is

SO amazed

and

impressed.

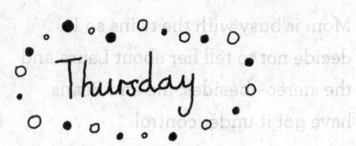

THIS IS IT. We are about to join the dots and solve our first case AND save Amy and the talent show!

Me and Beans go up to Mr. D.'s desk first thing. I give Beans a "you go first" look and he gives me a "no—YOU go first" look back.

"The thing is, Mr. D.," I say, "Laura

has a really mean plan to win the talent show by sabotaging Amy's song—I saw the stereo player in her bag at home time yesterday and I think—"

But at that moment Laura comes in. She is carrying a huge sparkly stereo about five times the size of the crumby school one.

"This is mine and it's very expensive, but I'm bringing it in for the talent show," she says, "for everyone to use! I tried the school one at home and it's definitely broken."

Oh.

She does her sweet smile that she uses in front of teachers.

"Thank you, Laura!" says Mr. D. Then he gives Beans and me a very stern look and sends us back to our seats.

This is not how Fred Fantastic's grand reveals end ... There is usually more clapping.

DOT HQ *Later that day, I think about how the stereo clue turned out to be* **A RED HERRING**. *This actually has nothing to do with fish ...*

It means it led us up the wrong path and we made a mistake.

✗ ✗ ✗ ✗ ✗
✗ ✗

I feel really bad about it. I have a comforting hug with McClusky.
But this doesn't mean Amy is safe.

The **CLOCK IS STILL TICKING**—*we are* **RUNNING OUT OF TIME**—*and* **THE STAKES ARE HIGH!** *That's what Fred Fantastic would say, anyway.*

But I don't know what to do next.

FRIDAY

All I can say about today is that
my tangerine rolled off my desk
and Frankie Logan stepped on it,
although it was an accident.
<u>N☺T</u> a good day.

Saturday

 Night-time. Woken up. It is pitch black and must be the middle of the night. I can hear a strange whirring sound coming from along the corridor.

whirrrrrrrrrrr

clunk

clunk

whirrrrrrrrrrr

clunk

What IS that noise?

I get out of bed, open my door and suddenly …

Mom pops her head out of her bedroom and says, "What on earth are you doing up, Dot?"

I tell her about the odd whirring noise—but by now it has stopped.

"Back into bed, young lady—you're just dreaming!" says Mom.

I put my head under my pillow and I am trying to get back to sleep. But now it feels as if my brain is whirring too. I wasn't imagining it.

WHAT IS GOING ON???

SUNDAY

Now there are TWO mysteries! At school there is the great **LAURA AND THE TALENT SHOW MYSTERY** and at home there is my missing photo and the funny night-time whirring.

This is like a really tricky join-the-dots puzzle, but try as I might they just don't connect at all.

And now I'm REALLY worrying about the talent show—how bad will it be???

At dinner time, Mom looks at me and says, "I think we all need ice-cream sundaes."

She gets out the tall glasses and long spoons, and soon the kitchen table is covered in toppings and sprinkles.

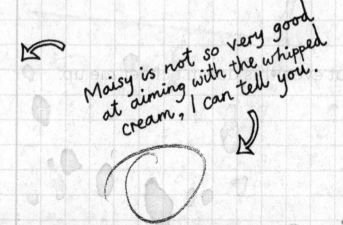

Maisy is not so very good at aiming with the whipped cream, I can tell you.

Alf picks out a pink sugar flower for me.

But even this doesn't cheer me up.

Monday

Putting one pink wafer in the chink.

I say to Beans, "We are no closer
to solving this case—and the talent
show is THIS THURSDAY! What
would Fred Fantastic do?"

"He'd say we need A LUCKY BREAK,"
says Beans. **"STAY FROSTY**, DOT!"

We spend ALL OF RECESS in The
Lookout (even though we miss our
class's turn on the ping-pong table)
and keep our eyes peeled.

Fred Fantastic would have coffee and
a bag of donuts on a stakeout.

Me and Beans only have half a bag of
chips to share.

And there is no sign of Laura doing
anything suspicious.

Still no new clues.

Still nothing.

One wafer in the chink, just to say there is nothing to say.

We break the wafer in two and miserably munch on our halves.

After dinner, I see ... another thing missing from my room! My blue polka-

127

dotted T-shirt that is a bit too small for me (OK it is size four years and I can't get my head through the head hole, but I still love it)—GONE!!!

Plus our TV is on the blink, so I miss **FRED FANTASTIC—ACE DETECTIVE**.

This is going from bad to worse!

My life is full of puzzles I just can't solve.

I guess I'm not as good a detective as I thought I was.

Wednesday

I bring the lucky shoes to school in a shoebox and give them to Amy to put in the props closet behind the stage.

She says in a really quiet voice, "These shoes are the only things making me feel brave enough to be in the talent show tomorrow."

"You are going to be GREAT!" I say to her.

But I am worried. I can't tell Amy that though—her nerves are already shredded.

Me and Beans finish our art project. I roll it up and put it in my bag.

 After dinner, I'm lying on my bed, having an emergency super-sour apple candy. I am utterly discombobulated— we have only a few hours left and I do not know what to do!

McClusky comes in with his squeaker...

... hoping to play.

Sorry, McClusky, I'm not in the mood.

He goes off around the room, exploring.
Now he's bringing me an old crumpled up
bit of paper. It's the first clue that wasn't
a clue, from behind the trash bin where I
threw it and missed.

No, McClusky, that's just nothing.

Not really thinking, I wipe off the dribble
and uncrumpled it and look.

Then I remember the **FRED FANTASTIC**
episode where he solves the whole case
with just half a bus ticket.

What if…?

What if this was half a message,
with some of the letters missing…?

What if this was a clue after all…?

I grab a pen and try out a few things.

No, that can't be it.

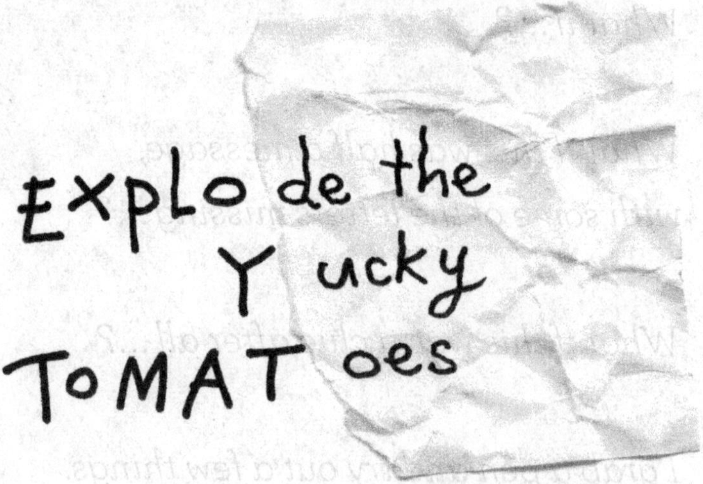

EXPLOde the
Yucky
ToMAToes

No, no, that can't be her plan, surely!

SLIde the
Ducky
Toes

Oh, this is **RIDICULOUS!**

We need a **LUCKY BREAK**, *as Fred Fantastic would say.*

Lucky break … lucky … shoes …

Hang on a minute …

LIGHT-BULB MOMENT!!!!!!

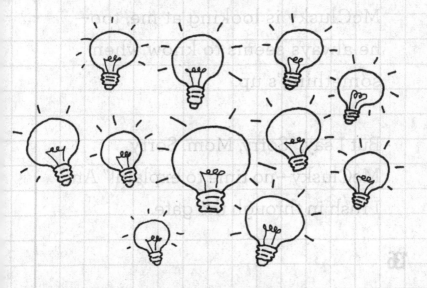

Thursday

I MAKE Mom take me and the twins
to school super-extra early. Mom
says, "Is everything OK, Dot?"

McClusky is looking at me, too—
he always seems to know when
something's up.

But I say, "Sorry, Mom. Sorry,
McClusky—no time to explain!" And
I rush in through the gate.

I put three wafers in the chink as I pass, which means **TOTALLY LIFE-AND-DEATH EMERGENCY COME STRAIGHTAWAY!!**

But Beans doesn't see it—Beans is not here! Amy remembers he has gone to the dentist. DISASTER!

In Math class, which is usually my favorite, I cannot concentrate AT ALL.

In quiet reading, I look at the same sentence over and over again, but I

am not even taking it in.

I WISH I could tell Mr. D., but after
last time when it all went so horribly
wrong, I don't dare.

And I can't think of ANY excuse to
check the props closet!

At recess, I sneak into the hall and
I'm just heading behind the stage
when Mr. Meades appears. He looks
at me suspiciously.

"Oh, Mr. Meades, I thought I could

help you with the sweeping!" I say
desperately, because it's the first
thing that pops into my head.

WHY DID I SAY THAT?!?! Now I am
spending all break with a huge broom.

Lunchtime—still no Beans.

Then just as class begins ... Beans
walks in! I try to whisper to him as
he sits down, but—

OH NO! Mr. D. suddenly sends me
and some of the other Support Crew

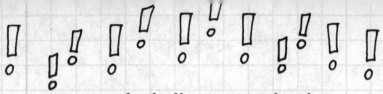

across to the hall to set up for the
talent show. He sends Beans to put
up decorations in the playground.

I make a "THIS IS AN EMERGENCY!"
face and Beans makes a "WHAT HAS
HAPPENED??" face. But we can't do
any more than that…

It is taking all afternoon to set up the
chairs. I cannot get away!

Now parents are arriving and Beans
is taking tickets and Mrs. Bagshott
gives me programs to hand out and I

STILL haven't told Beans about my
LIGHT-BULB MOMENT!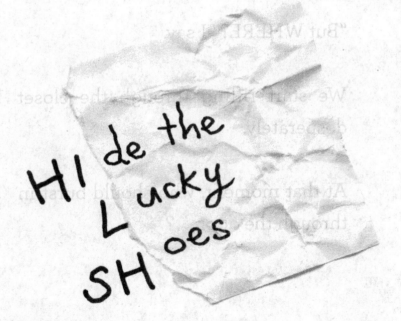

The show is just about to begin. In the
dark behind the stage, at last I get the
chance to show Beans the clue…

HIde the
Lucky
SHoes

We rush to the props closet. We look in the shoebox.

THE LUCKY SHOES ARE GONE.

"We must search!" says Beans.

"But WHERE?" I say.

We start rifling through the closet desperately.

At that moment, who should burst in through the door…?

McCLUSKY!!!!!!!!

He just somehow KNEW we needed him!

He must have escaped from home—Grandpa George is baby-sitting and dog-sitting tonight, but McClusky is way too quick for him.

McClusky sniffs the air and rushes back out of the door. Beans rushes after him.

But where are they going?

Mr. D. is calling, "Curtain up in ten seconds!" He glances over at the door with a surprised expression as it bangs shut behind Beans.

OH NO—here comes Amy! How can I distract her? Will she go onstage without the lucky shoes?

"Those shoes you are wearing already are LOVELY," I say. "That's my FAVORITE shade of black! Maybe you should wear them instead—red and sparkly is so last year…" I am babbling like a lunatic.

But it is too late. Amy is looking in the empty shoebox and her eyes go wide with shock.

Her bottom lip starts to wobble.

It's all a **horrible disaster.**

But then ... Beans and McClusky are rushing back in again!

And Beans is HOLDING THE SHOES!

"I was just polishing them!" Beans says to Amy.

"They were behind the playground equipment crate!" Beans whispers to me. "I remembered we saw Laura looking there!"

"Oh YES!" I say.

"But it was McClusky who sniffed them out under the soccer balls."

I pat McClusky on the head.

Amy is all smiles now.

WE DID IT! We high-five behind

Amy's back. "Good work, partner!"
I say.

We bustle McClusky into the props
closet before anyone ELSE sees
him —"Be quiet, McClusky!"—
because there is NO WAY a dog is
allowed in school.

What will Mr. D. say? No time to
worry about that now!

Amy puts on the shoes and...

THE SHOW BEGINS.

I slip around to the front and sit down next to Mom with a huge sigh of relief. "This is exciting!" says Mom.

Exciting is one way of putting it, I think to myself. If only she knew!

Beans sits next to me with his dad. He grins—he's thinking the same thing.

Kirstie is first with her tap dancing. She's fantastic—her feet are an absolute blur!

Next, Marcus is showing his amazing

yo-yo tricks. No one loses an eye, thank goodness.

There are lots more acts. Lots and LOTS. I like the really cool magic tricks, but there are an awful lot of recorders...

Then it's Laura. She makes a cross face at her backing singers every time they sing louder than her. None of them looks as if they're enjoying it.

But now I'm nervous again. Here comes Amy.

Laura has gone to sit in the audience.
I can see her looking in amazement
at Amy's feet—all red and sparkly.
She makes an angry "how did Amy
get the shoes back?!?!" face.

But even with my lucky shoes, Amy
looks very scared. OH DEAR.

The music starts, but Amy does not
sing.

Mr. D. stops the music, then starts it
again from the beginning. He gives
Amy an encouraging smile, but her

mouth still doesn't open.

Now Laura is sniggering.

It's horrible.
What should I do?
I can't just sit here…

Suddenly I have my **BIGGEST AND BEST LIGHT-BULB MOMENT EVER!**

I grab my bag from under my chair, and out of it I take our weather project—the rainbow banner Beans and I have

been making in art lessons for ages.
It is **VERY** long and **SO** bright and
glittery that sunglasses might be
recommended.

Deep breath. Then I jump up out of
my chair, on to the stage … and into
the spotlight with Amy.

Mom looks a bit surprised and I
can hear gasps and a huge **WHOOP**
from Beans.

I must be crazy! I'm no good at singing—and I haven't even got the lucky shoes on! But at least Amy is smiling. The music starts again.

Me and Amy hold an end of the banner each and we sing "Over the Rainbow" together. I can't remember all the words, but I am **LOUD!**

THEN from backstage we hear a loud whine, the crash of a

closet door flying open, and...

McClusky bursts on to the stage!

He howls loudly—he is singing, too!

This is his Toto moment!

So proud of you, Dot!
Love, Mom xx

We finish and burst out laughing.

EVERYBODY is cheering!

CORRECTION—everybody is cheering EXCEPT Laura.

At the end of the show, Mr. D. says, "A quick word, please, Dot."

OH NO. It will be about McClusky. Mom has taken him outside now, but he should not have been in school AT ALL—let alone in the talent show!

"What was all of that kerfuffle backstage before the show?" asks Mr. D.

I think about telling him everything. But it all worked out OK in the end —and now feels like the time for celebrating instead.

So I say that Amy's shoes went *missing* last minute, and that me and Beans *found* them just in time. And McClusky helped.

Mr. D. looks thoughtful, but all he says

is, "You helped a friend, Dot. That was a really, REALLY cool thing to do."

Now everybody is coming back into the hall …

The judges are announcing the winner!

And the winner is …

Fiyaz for his jokes!

Everyone is clapping loudly because Fiyaz is VERY funny.

CORRECTION—everyone is clapping EXCEPT Laura.

Amy claps the loudest. She is smiling and laughing and doesn't care at all about not winning.

I'm chatting with my new friends. Kirstie is teaching Amy and me some tap dancing, and Fiyaz is showing Beans how to raise one eyebrow.

Mom comes back in and gives me a big hug. Then she takes me and McClusky home. It's cold and getting dark and everything looks different with the streetlights on.

Grandpa George is very relieved to see McClusky. "He slipped past me when I was putting the rubbish out— such a mischievous guy!" he says.

We tell him all about the talent show and Grandpa gives me a big hug, too.

Then I go up to HQ...

AND I CANNOT BELIEVE MY EYES.

There are curtains … (So THAT was the funny whirring noise – Mom's sewing machine!)

There are homemade decorations … (My rainbow socks! My polka-dotted T-shirt!)

There's my photo of me and McClusky in a frame on the wall …

And a new **FRED FANTASTIC** puzzle book from the twins …

Dots everywhere …

AND A CHANDELIER!

I run back to Mom and give her a GINORMOUS hug.

"Thank you SO MUCH, Mom!" I say.
"I LOVE it!"

And that's almost the end of this
diary because—look!—there is hardly
any space left. But it is not QUITE
the end…

Friday

In class the next day, Mr. D. says,
"I have some announcements!

"Amy has been chosen to sing in
assembly next week. Well done, Amy!
Laura, if you like, you can do Amy's
backing vocals."

Mr. D. may have googly eyes, but I
don't think he misses much.

Then he says, "I also have two special certificates ... One for Dot and one for Beans—backstage superstars who can keep things on track and find crucial props in the most unlikely places EVER!"

BACKSTAGE SUPERSTAR

DOT!

BACKSTAGE SUPERSTAR

BEANS!

And I have something really special
for McClusky. Mom helped me order
it at the pet shop.

McClusky—
♡ TOP DOG detective! ♡

It is a brand-new tag for his collar, a
reward for sniffing out the vital clue
that saved the day.

So, the first case for the Join the Dots
Detectives is ...

But what will our next fiendishly
tricky mystery be ...?

Look out for more

coming soon in ...

DOTTY DETECTIVE AND THE GREAT PAWPRINT PUZZLE

Turn the page for a sneaky peek!

DETECTIVE

coming soon in ...

DOTTY DETECTIVE AND THE

SUNDAY

Something is odd and different at breakfast. Takes me a minute to realize what it is … the twins are really quiet. They ask Mom for a blanket.

"Are you two going down with a cold?" she asks and feels their foreheads.

Nice lazy afternoon. Watching a
movie with Mom.

Think I'll head to my room and get
ready for school tomorrow.

I'm just walking down the hallway,
and it's getting dark ...

... and I have the strangest feeling
that someone is behind me. But when
I turn around there's nobody there.

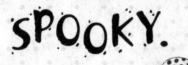

Bedtime. Nearly asleep, when—what's that??? There's a NOISE outside my room.

Tap-tappit

Tap-tappit ...

I pop my head around the door but the hallway is empty.

I know the twins are fast asleep by now, and I can hear Mom is on the phone in her room so it can't be her.

I RUSH back into bed. This is a mystery.

This is a case for the Join The Dots Detectives!

JOIN
THE DOTS
DETECTIVES

ON THE CASE